S0-ACL-215

OTHER YEARLING BOOKS YOU WILL ENJOY:

Whitey Ropes and Rides, GLEN ROUNDS

Ben and Me, ROBERT LAWSON

Mr. Revere and I, ROBERT LAWSON

Poor Richard in France, F. N. MONJO

The Clay Pot Boy, CYNTHIA JAMESON

Once Under the Cherry Blossom Tree, ALLEN SAY

Three Friends, ROBERT FREMLIN

Headlines, MALCOLM HALL

A Toad for Tuesday, RUSSELL E. ERICKSON

Blue Moose, MANUS PINKWATER

YEARLING BOOKS are designed especially to entertain and enlighten young people. The finest available books for children have been selected under the direction of Charles F. Reasoner, Professor of Elementary Education, New York University.

For a complete listing of all Yearling titles,
write to Education Sales Department, Dell Publishing Co., Inc.,
1 Dag Hammarskjold Plaza, New York, N.Y. 10017

Whitey & the Wild Horse

GLEN ROUNDS

WHITEY & the WILD HORSE

A YEARLING BOOK

Published by
Dell Publishing Co., Inc.
1 Dag Hammarskjold Plaza
New York, New York 10017

For information address Holiday House, Inc.,
New York, New York 10022.
Yearling ® TM 913705, Dell Publishing Co., Inc.
Reprinted by arrangement with Holiday House, Inc.
ISBN: 0-440-49620-9
Printed in the United States of America

Second Dell Printing —June 1979

Contents

From Eagle Butte 7

The Trap 23

Feed and Water 43

The Taming 55

The Wild Horse Hunter 69

From Eagle Butte

"I BET we could catch a wild horse, if we really tried," Josie remarked.

"What would we do with one if we caught him?" Whitey asked, looking up from the bottom of the pit where he was hunting for arrowheads.

"Tame him, of course," she answered. "Or maybe sell him."

"They're pretty hard to catch," Whitey said. "Besides, I don't think there are any around here."

7

"I know where there's one," Josie persisted. "He's grazing over there on the ridge right where we saw him yesterday."

"Oh!" Whitey scoffed. "That horse."

The horse they spoke of was a lone pinto they often saw from a distance as they prowled the broken country here along the River. Whitey climbed out of the pit and sprawled on the dry buffalo grass to watch the horse and consider the matter.

Catching wild horses wasn't a business that many fellows his age worked at. On the other hand, he'd been doing pretty much a man's work ever since he'd come to live on the ranch with Uncle Torwal, and that was for almost as long as he could remember. Besides, Uncle Torwal was always telling him

that the only way to find out if you could do a thing was to try it.

Of course, Josie was only a girl, but she was catching onto ranch business pretty well. She was his cousin, and since she had first come to the ranch, a year or so before, she had gotten to be right handy.

Between them, they helped Uncle Torwal with the work around the house: washing, cooking and other chores, as well as riding to look after stock. But even so, they had considerable free time for projects of their own. This high butte, with its caved-in pits where the Indians had once hidden to catch war eagles, was one of their favorite places.

"I don't think that's a wild horse," Whitey said at last.

"He looks as wild as any horse I ever saw," Josie said. "We haven't ever been able to get anywhere near him."

"He's wild that way, all right," Whitey agreed. "But he's a range horse, most likely, with someone's brand on him."

"There are wild horses around, aren't there?" Josie went on.

"There are some wild horses, sure," he explained as patiently as he could. "But mostly they are farther back in the Red Hills yonder, thirty or forty miles from here. Besides, wild horses are generally a runty, scrubby lot, and you wouldn't want one if you saw it."

They had been over this many times, but Josie was still sure that it would be a fine thing to catch and tame a wild horse.

They unwrapped their lunches and looked out over the country while they ate. It was so quiet that they could hear a fly buzzing in the grass a dozen yards away. As usual, there was a small breeze in this high place, making it pleasant in spite of the hot day. After they'd eaten they lay for a while watching the small clouds overhead. Then Whitey went back into the eagle pits to hunt again for arrow-heads.

Down there, he thought about being an Indian hidden under a carefully woven cover of grass, waiting for an eagle to see the wolf liver bait staked nearby. In his mind he watched the circling eagle, wondering if the mat covering the pit looked enough like the rest of the grass to fool the bird. He thought of how the Indian must feel, after being cramped and motionless there since before daylight, when he saw the great war bird begin to spiral closer and closer. Whitey could almost see the bright yellow eye examining every blade of grass around the wolf carcass and the liver showing through a slash in the furry side.

The picture became more real. When the eagle finally lighted on the ground and started tearing at the bait, Whitey began to wonder at the nerve it would take to reach out and catch the taloned legs with bare hands. Old-timers had told of how the flapping, screaming bird was hauled down into the cramped hole with the hunter, and its life

crushed out against the side of the pit. It was a risky business, for the golden eagle is a powerful bird, and beak, wings, and talons are all vicious weapons.

The picture was so real that Whitey came up with a start when Josie's call came suddenly to him.

"Whitey! There is something queer moving over across the River. Come see what it is."

It took Whitey a little bit to get loose from his eagle-catching dream, but when Josie kept insisting, he clambered out of the pit and looked where she was pointing.

"It's beyond the first little ridge the other side of the River," she told him. "Just about over the top of that white cottonwood snag."

After watching a while, Whitey said, "I don't see anything."

"Wait a minute! It goes out of sight and then comes back. There!"

"I see it now, I think. Looks like some kind of animal jumping around."

"That's it," she told him. "It's been doing that off and on for quite a while. What could it be?"

For a long time they watched the strange movement. Sometimes it would appear, only to go out of sight again almost at once. Other times it stayed in view for a minute or two.

"It stays in the same place all the time," Whitey remarked at last.

"Maybe it's a coyote, or a wolf," Josie suggested. "Or maybe a mountain lion, even!"

"No," Whitey disagreed, "it's too dark colored for any of them. It's almost black. Might be a dog; looks about that size."

They continued to watch, hoping the thing might come farther out into the open so they could tell for sure what it was.

"It might be a dog caught in a trap," Whitey said, after the thing had appeared and disappeared several times more in the same place. "He could be in a little washout so that we only see him when he lunges uphill against the chain.

"Or it might be a man laying in high grass waving a jacket to attract attention," he went on.

"What would he be laying in the grass for?" Josie wanted to know.

"He might have been thrown, or had his horse fall and hurt him," Whitey explained. "There are a dozen things it might be."

By this time they were both feeling uneasy about the whole thing.

After a while Whitey said, "Maybe we'd better go and take a look."

"Do you think we should?" Josie asked doubtfully. "It might be dangerous."

"I don't know what would be dangerous about it," he answered. "If it is a man and he's hurt it might be days before anyone else found him."

"That's a sort of deserted country over there, for a fact. Even if it's only a dog in a trap, I guess we should find out about it," Josie agreed.

They dawdled, half dreading to go, and hoping they'd see somebody else riding this way. Maybe the thing would go away. That was badlands country, there across the River. They'd always been a little afraid to go into it.

Finally they did climb down the steep sides of the butte to where their horses were tied. After straightening the saddle blankets and tightening the cinches, they mounted and rode slowly toward the River.

The Trap

AT THIS time of year the River was only a narrow, shallow trickle winding through wild flats of sand and gravel. But huge, sun-whitened trunks of dead cottonwood trees, their tangled roots reaching high in the air, told of the power of the flood season. Flood trash still lodged high in the branches of the straggly trees lining the River's edge. It was not a particularly cheerful place, and Whitey and Josie did not stop there any longer than it took for their horses to drink.

23

Afterwards they rode through the straggling band of cottonwoods and on up the slope to the first low ridge beyond. Reining up their horses, they looked about them.

Ahead for several hundred yards was a stretch of ground cut in all directions by deep gullies and washouts. Flash floods pouring down the wide coulees beyond had made a miniature badlands of the soft soil.

A flood's force pouring over the lip of a cut-bank often scooped out deep steep-sided potholes below. The potholes increased in size with each passing flood until some were as much as eight or ten feet deep and twenty or thirty feet across. Well-worn stock trails wound in and out between the washouts.

Whitey and Josie waited and watched for

several minutes. A golden eagle circled lazily overhead, and a file of sage hens clucking softly marched down a path towards the River. But except for them they saw or heard nothing that was out of the ordinary.

Thinking they might have come to the wrong place, they rode cautiously along the stock trails first in one direction and then in another. In places the trail gave out a hollow sound beneath their horses' hoofs, for flood water, eating away a softer streak, had hollowed out passages underneath the trails. It was not surprising that they felt uneasy riding through the place.

After they'd stopped to listen several times, Whitey said, "Guess maybe it wasn't anything, after all. We might as well go."

Josie agreed. "That suits me. I don't like this place."

Then they heard a sound. It was a muffled thumping, seeming to come from somewhere almost underfoot.

Startled, Josie looked at Whitey.

"It must be coming from down in one of the washouts," he said, sliding off his horse.

Josie did the same, and leaving the horses with the reins dropped, they started looking around the heads of the gullies. It was hard to tell exactly where the sound was coming from.

And then, besides the thumping noise, they heard a heavy wheezy noise, something between a whistle and a hiss. They stopped and looked uneasily at each other.

"It must be an animal of some kind," Whitey said. "But I never heard one like it."

Josie pulled at his sleeve. "I don't think we'd better go any closer. Let's get Uncle Torwal to bring his .30-.30."

"I'd like to find out what it is, first," Whitey replied.

But he made no move to go closer to the disturbance that seemed to be coming from down in the ground not far ahead of them. After a little the thumping noises stopped, and the curious wheezings almost died away also.

"I'm going a little closer while it's quieted down," Whitey whispered, and moved on tiptoe a few steps.

Josie followed him, just as quietly. They'd

move stealthily a little way, and then stop to listen before going on again. The soft wheezing rose and fell but didn't seem any nearer.

"Whatever it is—" Josie started to say, when a commotion almost under their feet interrupted her. The strange breathing suddenly grew loud and the ground trembled a little from the weight of some heavy body, while an unrecognizable black shape jumped out of the ground just ahead, and quickly disappeared again.

For a moment they were too startled to speak, and then the shape came up again.

"It's a horse!" Whitey exclaimed. "He's trying to get out of a washout!"

They moved ahead carefully so as not to frighten the horse more than necessary.

Soon they could look down into a pothole fifteen or twenty feet across and seven or eight feet deep. In the bottom was a black horse, backed against the far side, watching them.

For a while they and the horse watched each other, and there was no sound except the heavy labored breathing.

"How did he get there, do you suppose?" Josie asked after a bit.

At the sound of her voice the horse lunged back against the bank, making the thudding noise they had heard before, and the sound of his breathing grew louder.

Whitey whispered, "He must have been chased by something, or else he was crowded over the edge by the rest of a bunch. His hind leg is hurt, too. See how it hangs."

Josie whispered back, "Do you think it's broken?"

"Hard to tell," Whitey told her. "From the way the leg swings it may be in the stifle joint."

The trampled floor of the pothole made it plain that the horse had been in there a day or two. His eyes were sunken and his ribs showed through his black hide. He was plastered with dirt, and patches of dried blood caked several skinned places on his back and shoulders.

"His nose is all swelled up," Josie noticed. "Do you suppose he's been snake-bitten?"

Whitey had been wondering about that, too. Now he saw something else. "His nostrils have been wired. That's what makes him breathe so hard," he told her.

"What do you mean?" Josie wanted to know.

"Just that," answered Whitey. "It's a thing wild horse catchers sometimes do so they can handle them easier. They cut a little slit in either side of the nostril and run a piece of bale wire through from side to side to partly close the horse's nose and shut off his wind. As long as he does no more than walk or trot a little he's all right, but as soon as he tries to run he chokes down."

"Then he is a wild horse!" Josie cried.

"I guess so," Whitey agreed. "He doesn't seem to have any brand on him, and Uncle Torwal said there were some horse hunters working back by the Black Hawk Buttes country."

"But how did he get here?" Josie persisted.

"They must have been driving a bunch through the country," Whitey explained patiently. "Perhaps this one broke away while they were having trouble with the others, and they didn't know where he'd gone when he fell in here out of sight."

Looking carefully around, they found the horse's tracks coming in great leaps down the slope, straight to the caved-in bank. And on the flat above they found tracks showing where a considerable band of horses had been driven past.

Back at the edge of the pothole they con-

sidered the problem. There was no way they could get the horse out, for at the lowest place the banks were higher than their heads.

"Could we cave the bank down enough so that he could come out by walking up the pile of dirt?" Josie wondered.

"Hard and dry as the ground is, it would be a big job, even with a pick and a crowbar," Whitey answered. "If his leg wasn't crippled it might be done, but he couldn't possibly scramble up the way he is."

"But if he stays there much longer he'll starve to death," Josie said.

"Or die of thirst," Whitey added. "But if we tell Uncle Torwal he'll come and shoot him to put him out of his misery."

For a long time they sat unhappily watching the imprisoned horse.

At last Josie said, "He is mighty handsome. It seems a shame he has to be shot, especially after all the trouble he's had getting away from the wild horse hunters."

"Yeah," agreed Whitey.

It was getting late in the afternoon, so they reluctantly left the wild horse and started riding slowly back to the ranch.

After a long silence Josie asked, "Who owns him now?"

"Anyone that finds him, I guess," Whitey answered.

"You mean that if we could get him out and tame him we could keep him?"

"I imagine so, but I don't see how we could do either one," Whitey said.

"Why couldn't we carry water to him from the River and cut grass for him and keep him alive until we figured a way to get him out? Maybe if we were kind to him he'd be tame after his leg got well, and we could keep him!"

Whitey did not reply, and for a while they both rode silently, thinking about the possibility. Then Whitey stopped his horse.

"It would be an awful lot of work, and we'd have to keep it a secret," he said.

"But that's a way to get a wild horse of our own!" Josie insisted. "Besides, he's too fine a horse to be shot."

After some more talk, they decided not to say anything to Uncle Torwal about the horse for a while at least. It was too late to do anything about him that day, but first thing in the morning they'd see what they could do.

All the rest of the way home they discussed plans.

After supper, while Uncle Torwal read the paper, Whitey and Josie hurried with the dishes, carried in a fresh bucket of water, and filled the woodbox for morning. Then they went down to the windmill and sat on the edge of the horse trough to discuss plans again.

"First thing, we have to find a wooden tub, and figure some way to get it over there in the morning," Whitey said.

"Why couldn't we just take a bucket for him to drink out of?" Josie asked. "It would be lots easier."

"The rattle of it would scare him, if nothing else," Whitey explained. "And besides, he'd more than likely tip it over if he did try to drink out of it."

They decided that the old wood tub in the blacksmith shop would be just the thing. Besides that, they'd need a bucket to carry water in, and the old handsickle for cutting grass.

By the time they'd settled on those things it was bedtime, and they were sure they'd never be able to sleep for thinking of the trapped horse.

Feed and Water

THE NEXT morning they were up and about before Uncle Torwal had the fire started in the stove. In spite of their impatience, they had to act as if there was nothing special on their minds.

When breakfast and the few morning chores were done they saddled their horses. Then they had to wait around until Uncle Torwal left before gathering their things together. Otherwise he'd be sure to ask what they wanted with all that stuff. This was his

43

day for going to town, but it seemed that he never would get started.

But at last he did, and just before he rode out the gate he asked, "What you fellers planning on doing today?"

After a minute's thought Whitey answered, "Why, we kinda thought we might go wild horse hunting."

Uncle Torwal looked a little startled, but he was pretty well used to the odd things they tried now and then, so he only remarked, "Well, I hope you catch one," and rode away.

Before he was out of sight, Whitey had rolled the wooden tub out of the blacksmith shop, and Josie had got the bucket and sickle. Then they went for their horses.

"How are we going to carry the stuff?" Josie wanted to know.

"I don't know, yet," Whitey told her.

They tried to figure some way to fasten the tub to a saddle, but no matter how they tried it, it wouldn't balance. And it was too heavy to hang on the horse's side.

"We'll have to haul it on the old stoneboat," Whitey decided.

The stoneboat was a rough sled-like contraption used around the ranch for hauling water barrels. Whitey fastened one end of his rope to it and the other end to the saddle horn. Then he pulled the stoneboat around to the tub.

When everything was loaded they rode out across the pasture. It was slow going, for

the old stoneboat seemed to catch on every
sage bush or clump of bunch grass. Old Spot
grumbled and groaned at the load, although
it wasn't really hard to pull. Now and again
the tub fell off, and there was a great rattle
and clatter from the bucket and the sickle.
But in spite of all, it was still early when they
came to the River.

Stopping after they had forded the shallow stream, they got off their horses and used
the bucket to dip water and fill the tub.

Then they started on again, anxious to see
how the wild horse was doing, and to get the
water to him. Spot groaned as usual when he
felt the drag of the stoneboat, but it moved
only a few inches and then dug itself into the
gravel and stopped.

Josie got down and kicked away the rocks that had piled up in front of it, and Whitey spoke to Spot again. Soon they realized that he couldn't pull the load when the tub was full of water. There was nothing to do but empty it and then refill it after they were out on the firm ground again.

By the time they had finally come near the washout they were plastered with sweat and dirt. Leaving the horses a little distance off, they went carefully forward to see how the wild horse was doing.

He was standing backed against the far side just as they'd left him. But the deep tracks showed where he'd gone round and round the walls of his prison during the night, trying to get out. After watching them a little while he dropped his head until his nose almost touched the ground. Every now and again he chomped his jaws and made rasping noises with his tongue.

"He needs water bad," Whitey said.

They hurried to drag the stoneboat close to the edge of the bank. A big part of the water had sloshed out, in spite of their care on the way from the River. Even so, it took all their strength to get the tub off the stoneboat. Until then they hadn't thought how they'd get the tub of water down the bank to where the horse could get at it. Now they saw that it couldn't be done.

"We can drop the tub over all right after it's empty. We'll have to fill the bucket and pour the rest out," Whitey decided.

They poured the water that was left down the bank, hoping the smell of it might keep the horse from being afraid of the tub. But when it struck the bottom, the horse came to life again and fought the banks so violently they were afraid he would do more damage to his injured leg.

It was something of a trick to lean out far enough to pour the bucket of water into the tub below, but they managed it. After that they went to get more water from the River.

At first they tried hauling with the stone-boat, but the full bucket sloshed and tipped until they decided there was nothing to do but walk and carry it. Even taking turns, it was hard work, and they made a dozen trips before the tub was full.

Then, flopping down on the grass, they
rested awhile and watched the horse. He
stood against the side of the pothole, as far
from the tub as he could get.

"He hasn't tried to drink, yet," Josie said.

"The tub is a strange thing to him, and it
may take quite a while before he gets up
courage to go near it," Whitey explained.
"Let's leave him alone and go cut some
grass."

The grass cutting was much easier than
the water hauling had been, and in a little
while they had several big armloads piled up.
When they carried them to the horse they
found him still standing against the far side
of the pothole. Wild as he was, there was no
way they could coax him to drink or eat.

They couldn't bear to go away and leave him. So for a long time they sat on the grass, making no sound and hoping that the horse would forget they were there and come to drink. But when he continued to stand facing them with no sign of relaxing, they finally realized that they had better leave him. So at last they got on their horses and rode off towards the ranch.

The Taming

WHEN Whitey and Josie hurried away next morning to saddle their horses, Uncle Torwal grinned and asked, "Going wild horse hunting again?"

"Yessir!" they said, figuring he'd be really surprised if he knew that was exactly what they were doing.

They found the horse standing in the same place as before, but the tub was almost empty. From the size of the patch of mud on the ground it was plain enough that most of the water had leaked out through the cracks be-tween the dried staves. But the horse had damp mud on his muzzle, so they figured he must have drunk at least a little. When they spoke softly to him he raised his head and watched them.

Refilling the tub wasn't such a problem as it had been yesterday, for Whitey had brought three canvas water bags. It was a simple matter to haul them on the stoneboat; they had corks and didn't slop over like a bucket.

The cut grass they'd thrown into the hole seemed to still be all there, but nonetheless they cut more. These chores took only a short time. Afterwards they sat talking to the horse and admiring him. His leg was still greatly

swollen and swung at odd angles when he moved, but the swelling in his nose seemed to have gone down a little.

"He's been rubbing his muzzle in the mud, and that seems to take some of the fever out. Helps keep the flies off, too," Whitey explained.

"Ugh!" Josie made a face, then added, "what about the wires? Is there any way we can get them out?"

"Not now," Whitey told her. "But they may come loose of themselves after a bit."

"How do you mean?"

"It's like a cactus thorn in your finger," Whitey told her. "You've had them fester a little and then come out by themselves. If the slits at the edge of his nostrils are not too deep they'll do the same thing, then slough away and let the wires drop off."

"What about his leg? Will it get well, do you think?" Josie asked.

"We'll have to wait and see. If it doesn't we'll never be able to get him out."

Every day, from then on, their routine was much the same. One way or another they found an excuse to leave the ranch early every morning, and were usually gone most of the day. If Uncle Torwal noticed anything unusual going on he said nothing about it.

At first the horse never drank the water or touched the grass while they were about, but every morning they found the tub empty and the grass eaten. Later they started bringing him bundles of carrots and other green things

from the ranch. Each day they spent long hours talking softly to him. The swelling in his leg went down little by little, and before long he would occasionally rest a little weight on the tip of that hoof.

As he became more and more used to them, they would sometimes find him with his head thrown up, waiting for his feed. One morning he whinnied while they were still some distance off, and they were filled with pride.

Josie cried, "He's lonesome for us! He's getting tame!"

"Looks like it," agreed Whitey, with a pleased grin.

As soon as they refilled the tub and sat still on the bank above, the horse came cautiously up to drink. It was a thing he'd never done before.

"Maybe he'll take a carrot from my hand," Josie whispered. Lying flat on her stomach, she held one out as far over the edge as she could reach. The horse stood a little way off, sniffing and pointing his ears, but wouldn't come that close.

From then on, every day Josie coaxed him with fresh carrots. One morning after many false starts, snuffing, and questioning with his sharp-pointed delicate ears, the horse reached far out, wrapped his soft upper lip over the carrot and took it gently from her fingers.

From then on his gentling proceeded rapidly. After carrots she tried sugar, which he didn't care for at first. But he soon learned to take the lump and work it with his tongue. After a few tastes he'd come back and blow his warm breath on her hand, looking for more. From that it was a simple matter to teach him to eat oats, which they brought from the ranch.

But all their dealings were still from the top of the bank. Then one morning, before they had poured in the fresh water, Whitey decided it was time he cleaned out the tub. By now enough mud had collected in it to make the water foul and murky looking.

He said to Josie, "I believe he'd let me go down and clean it out. Be ready to grab my hand and help me back up in a hurry."

Sliding carefully down the bank, Whitey

slowly tipped the tub and sloshed the remaining water around to sluice out the dirt.

The horse backed to the far corner of the pothole, watching nervously, but beyond that made no move. When Whitey finished he spoke to Josie.

"Hand me a carrot. I want to see if he'll come up to me."

Holding the carrot out, he talked quietly to the horse, who sniffed and moved his feet restlessly. After considering the matter a while, he came slowly closer until he could reach out and take it.

After that Whitey and Josie spent almost every daylight hour with their horse. Little by little he lost his fear of them, so that instead of talking to him from the top of the bank

they went down into the washout with him. Gradually he let them pet him and stroke his neck while he ate.

With a short piece of rope they began brushing dried mud out of his coat. After he became accustomed to that they would let the free end drop around his feet or slip lightly over his neck until he paid no more attention to it.

The wires holding the horse's nostrils shut were still in place, and his labored wheezing was painful to listen to. So Whitey brought a pair of wire cutters from the blacksmith shop. Working carefully while the horse tried to nuzzle a lump of sugar from between Josie's fingers, Whitey managed to snip both loops and partly straighten them.

Next day when they came back, the horse had gotten rid of both wires by rubbing his muzzle against the bank. The scars soon healed, but he would always carry the wild horse hunter's mark.

Without the wires to worry him, the horse improved even faster than before. His coat began to smooth out, and he seemed pleased by the attention he was getting.

One day Whitey brought a hackamore from the ranch. When he and Josie cautiously slipped the noseband over the horse's muzzle and eased the headpiece over his ears, he seemed more puzzled than frightened. For a while he tried to rub it off, but soon lost interest and paid no more attention to it.

The Wild Horse Hunter

AS SOON AS they were sure that the horse's leg was going to heal all right, Whitey and Josie began to figure how they would get him out of the hole when the time came. The only thing they could think of was to cave dirt down from one of the banks until they had a slope the horse could scramble up.

They brought a crowbar and a shovel from the ranch, but made little headway digging in the dry, hard ground. There was no great hurry, for the best slope they could make would be too steep for the horse to climb until his leg was entirely well. Besides, he seemed fairly content there and was getting more gentle each day.

So far the weather had been dry, but one afternoon black clouds started to pile up in the west, promising storm. All afternoon and evening Whitey and Josie watched it anxiously.

A little rain would maybe soften the ground and make the digging easier, but such clouds could bring one of the sudden heavy rains that turned the dry gullies into roaring streams. Such flash floods usually passed as quickly as they came, but that would be no help to their horse, trapped in the deep pothole. The chances were he

would drown before the water soaked away.

However, only a light rain fell, and by bedtime the sky was clear and the stars were out.

They worked hard every day at the digging, but it went slowly. They were not used to such tools. Every cloud was now a threat, and they watched the weather as they never had before.

One night just before supper a stranger rode into the ranch. After talking to Uncle Torwal a while, he unsaddled and turned his horse into the corral. Listening to the talk as they helped get supper, Josie and Whitey learned that he was Highpockets McCollum, the wild horse hunter.

All during supper Highpockets told tales

of how he went about his business. He explained that most of the horses were not the fancy wild ones of the movies, but scrubby things good only to be shipped east to be made into feed for fox farms and such.

The more they listened to him, the less Whitey and Josie liked him.

After supper Uncle Torwal suggested he stay over night, but the wild horse hunter said no.

"I have to see a fellow in town tomorrow morning about buying some horses," he said, "and in the afternoon I want to look for a horse I lost a while back."

"What kind of horse was it you lost?" Uncle Torwal asked, to be polite.

"He was with my last bunch of wild ones,"

Highpockets told him. "He must have been the colt of some range mare that ran off with the wild bunch. A big black horse worth some money.

"He broke away when I was bringing the bunch across Prairie Dog Flats on the way to the railroad. I couldn't leave the rest, to run him down. The chances are he went to water somewhere along the River. I had his nose wired, so he wouldn't go far."

Uncle Torwal remarked, "Probably be in pretty bad shape by this time if he's alive at all."

"Oh, it's hard to kill one of them horses," the hunter said, indifferently. "I'd like to find him, but if he's dead it ain't much loss —just another wild horse!"

And gathering his reins and thanking Uncle Torwal for supper, he rode off.

As soon as he left, Uncle Torwal went in the house to read his paper and Whitey and

Josie went down to the windmill to talk things over.

"He will find him!" Josie exclaimed. "There's a plain trail from the River where we've been hauling water in the stoneboat. Anybody riding that way is bound to wonder about it."

"And besides," Whitey added, "now that the horse is getting tame, he whinnies every time he hears anyone ride up."

They agreed they'd have to get the horse out before the man came back, if they wanted to save him.

"His leg is about all right, but will we have time to break that bank down enough to get him out?" Josie asked.

"Guess we'll have to see," Whitey replied.

For a while they just sat and worried, saying nothing.

Then Josie had a suggestion. "Maybe we should tell Uncle Torwal. He could help us get him out."

Whitey agreed. "Yes, but he might say we'd have to give the horse back—being as Uncle Torwal found him *after* Mr. McCollum had told about losing a horse."

"But we found him *before*—when he was truly lost. So he was really a wild horse, wasn't he?" Josie asked.

"Something like that," Whitey answered. "And if we get him out before the man comes back there will be no argument about it."

"If we can't get him out, we can still come

back and get Uncle Torwal later in the morning," he added. "But it wouldn't be like bringing him home ourselves."

AS THEY rode out of the corral gate next morning Whitey said, "I hope that wild horse hunter stays away all day in town."

The sun was only just coming up over the bluffs across the River, but they had already finished their outside chores and helped Uncle Torwal wash up the breakfast dishes. They needed every minute of the morning for the work ahead, if they were to save the horse.

As Whitey and Josie rode along, the grazing cattle raised their heads to look, and shiny red and white calves got lazily up from their naptime places in the grass to watch them pass. Farther on, prairie dogs were busy about their affairs, but took time to sit up on their burrow mounds and bark at them. A coyote trotted unafraid across a flat ahead. But for once they paid no attention to any of these things.

The wild horse whinnied as usual when he heard them coming. While they watered him and fed him carrots he fidgeted around restlessly, showing little sign of lameness.

But they had no time to visit with him. They scraped and dug at the hard ground, or tried to loosen it with the heavy crowbar. The horse watched them curiously.

Sweat ran into their eyes and their hands blistered, but progress was slow. By the middle of the morning they had lowered the bank only about a foot. At that rate it would take them days to get the horse out.

They climbed up onto the grass to rest a little and cool off. Lying on their backs, they talked a little of what to do. It began to look as though they'd have to give up and go back for Uncle Torwal.

About that time they heard the soft creak of saddle leather behind them, and jumped to their feet, startled. A little distance off they saw Uncle Torwal on his horse.

"Just happened to be riding this way, and saw you digging. Sort of wondered if you needed any help," he remarked mildly, as he got off his horse and squatted down on his boot heels.

"Well, we have a wild horse here," Whitey told him.

"Only he's not really wild, any more!" Josie added. "We've got him tamed, and if we can get him out of that washout before the wild horse hunter finds him we are going to save him."

"Is that a fact?" Uncle Torwal said. He didn't seem to be particularly surprised.

While he sat there they told him the whole story, of how they'd found the horse and kept him fed and watered, until now his leg was well, and he was tame besides. To prove it, Josie slid down to the horse and petted him while he rubbed his nose over her shirt and nibbled at her braids.

"I see you got a hackamore on him. Will

he lead?" Uncle Torwal asked, and stood up.

"Yessir, look!" Josie led him the few steps in any direction that there was space for.

"Well," Uncle Torwal remarked. "I see you were making a place to take him out. Let's get busy an' finish the business."

Picking up the crowbar, he started prying big chunks of hard dirt loose from the bank they'd been hacking at. In a few minutes he'd caved off enough to make a steep slope. Then the three of them worked at the pile of loose dirt, making sure it was firm enough to hold the horse's weight.

Uncle Torwal wiped sweat and dirt off his face with his sleeve saying, "Well, git your string on him an' lead him out. We'll soon find out if he's gentle or not."

Whitey and Josie went down and tied their rope to the hackamore. After talking to the horse a little, they turned him to face the pile of dirt and the broken side of the wall.

"Let him take his time, so he can see what he's getting into," Uncle Torwal told them.

The horse put his ears forward and snorted at the loose dirt. They coaxed him ahead little by little until with a snort and a lunge he leaped up the slope and came out on top.

Josie and Whitey both lost their feet on the slope, and the rope as well, so now their horse was out on the level with nothing but the trailing rope to hold him. And they were in the pothole. Uncle Torwal sat still and watched.

The horse trotted off some distance and

turned, snorting. Whitey was the first out of
the pothole. He moved quietly to the sack of
carrots, taking one of the two that were left
and giving one to Josie as she came up.

Talking softly, they moved out towards
the horse. When he nervously moved away
they stopped and went no farther. After a
few undecided circlings the horse finally
came up to them and stood quietly eating the
carrots while they petted him.

"It looks like you've got a horse, sure
enough," Uncle Torwal remarked after a
while. As they led the horse up to him he
added, "Looks like we got company, too."

It was the wild horse hunter, who had rid-
den up while they had been busy with the
horse.

"I see you caught my horse for me," Highpockets McCollum said, as he got off his horse and swaggered over.

"These young ones caught a horse," Uncle Torwal answered. "A handsome one, too, isn't he?"

"Sure he's a nice one," the hunter said. "That's why I was looking for him. He's my horse, all right. See the scars where I wired his nostrils?"

"Yeah, I particularly noticed them," Uncle Torwal said. "But these two found him in that hole, and if it hadn't been for them he'd have been dead long ago. They've fed an' watered him every day for over a month. Looks to me like they've tamed themselves a wild horse."

"But he's mine, I tell you, and he's a valuable horse." Highpockets insisted.

"I don't see any brand on him," Uncle Torwal remarked. "You told me yourself he was a wild horse you caught and let get away again—so the way I look at it he's still a wild horse."

"Well, if that's the way you feel about it, I'll buy him back," the hunter said, sulkily.

"You'll have to talk to them," Uncle Torwal told him, jerking his thumb to where Whitey and Josie were holding the horse's rope and listening.

Before the man had a chance to speak, Whitey said, "He's not for sale—"

Josie spoke up, interrupting, "We're going to make a saddle horse of him and maybe teach him tricks."

"Looks to me like you got competition in the wild horse business," Uncle Torwal said to Highpockets. "Better come on home with us and eat dinner."

But the wild horse hunter didn't seem to hear him. He grumpily said goodbye, and got on his horse and rode off.

After watching him go, Uncle Torwal remarked, "Gettin' about dinner time. Reckon you can get that horse home and put him in the corral without losin' him like that feller done?"

"Yessir!" Whitey and Josie said together.